THE STORY OF THE WNBA

BY ELLEN LABRECQUE

Four-time champion Maya Moore of the Minnesota Lynx

The Child's World®
childsworld.com

Published by The Child's World®
1980 Lookout Drive • Mankato, MN 56003-1705
800-599-READ • www.childsworld.com

Photographs:
Cover: Bill Kostroun/AP Images.
Interior: AP Images: Nam Y. Huh 5; Eric Draper, 6; Kevork Djansezian 9; Elaine Thompson 21. Newscom: Jeff Wheeler/TNS 2; Mike Cardew/KRT 10; Mike Zito/SportsChrome 13; Quinn Harris/Icon Sportswire 14; Anthony Nesmith/Cal Sport Media 17; Kevin Reece/Ai Wire 18.

ISBN 9781503835306
LCCN 2019944743

Printed in the United States of America

Contents

The World's Best!

Where do the world's best women's basketball players play? The WNBA! The Women's National Basketball Association tipped off in 1997. The league started its 24th season in 2020. The WNBA has included amazing players and memorable games. The league has **inspired** millions of young fans, too. How did it all happen? Here's the story of the WNBA.

Basketball fans young and old have enjoyed WNBA action for nearly 25 seasons. This fan shows her love for the Chicago Sky.

Shoot The Ball
We
SKY!

USA
13
USA
9

The Olympics

The WNBA *really* began with the 1996 Summer Olympics in Atlanta, Georgia. The US women's basketball team went 8–0. The Americans crushed their **opponents** by an average of 28 points per game. More than 25,000 people saw each game. After the Olympics, fans wanted to see these women play more! Two new **pro** leagues began right after the Olympics.

August 3, 1996: The US women's basketball team beats Brazil 111–87 for the gold medal at the Summer Olympics in Atlanta, Georgia.

United States teammates Rebecca Lobo (13) and Lisa Leslie won a gold medal!

Two Leagues

The American Basketball League (ABL) tipped off in the fall of 1996. The WNBA started in the summer of 1997. The ABL only lasted two seasons. On the other hand, the WNBA became a big success. **Center** Yolanda "Yo Yo" Griffith started with the ABL. With other ABL stars, she joined the WNBA in 1999. Players like Yo Yo made the WNBA bigger and better.

June 21, 1997: The WNBA's first game is played. The New York Liberty defeat the Los Angeles Sparks 67–57.

By 1997, US teammates Leslie and Lobo were playing each other in the WNBA.

SPARKS
9
50

34
WNBA

The First Champs

The WNBA went from saying "We got next," to "We got game." In the first season, the league attracted close to 10,000 fans per game. The biggest story was **guard** Cynthia Cooper of the Houston Comets. Cooper led the league in scoring, averaging 22.2 points per game. The Comets defeated the New York Liberty 65–51 in the first WNBA Championship Game. Cooper was named the first WNBA **MVP**.

In hoops, players waiting their turn to join pickup games say, "We got next!"

The Cleveland Rockers and Utah Starzz were two of the league's first eight teams.

And Three More

The Houston Comets ruled the early years of the WNBA. In 1998, they won 27 of 30 games. That is still the best record in WNBA history! Houston was led by three great players—Cynthia Cooper, Sheryl Swoopes, and Tina Thompson. Together, they helped the Comets win four titles in a row. Cooper was named the WNBA Finals MVP all four of those years.

August 26, 2000: The Houston Comets defeat the New York Liberty, two games to zero, to win their fourth WNBA title in a row.

Cooper is the WNBA's all-time leader in scoring. She averaged 20.1 points per game.

Comets
14
WNBA

ACES
22
UChicago
Medicine
14

More and More Teams

Eight teams played in the WNBA's first season. By 2019, 12 teams played in the league. Over the years, 18 different teams have played in the WNBA. Six teams moved to different cities, and six other teams stopped playing. The last team to move was the San Antonio Stars. They relocated to Nevada in 2017. They are now called the Las Vegas Aces.

July 30, 2002: Lisa Leslie of the Los Angeles Sparks throws down the first dunk in a WNBA game.

A'ja Wilson is the star of the Las Vegas Aces, the WNBA's newest team.

For the Record

Some WNBA records seem unbreakable. Guard Becky Hammon of the San Antonio Stars set a **free throw** record in 2014. She made all 35 of her shots without a single miss! Diana Taurasi of the Phoenix Mercury holds 10 WNBA records. One of them is for most career points. Since she joined the WNBA, she has scored more than 8,500 points! She is still scoring more and has no plans to retire anytime soon.

June 13, 2006: Fans vote for the first WNBA All-**Decade** Team. The list includes star players such as guard Sue Bird of the Seattle Storm and Cynthia Cooper of the Houston Comets.

After she stopped playing, Hammon became the first woman to be an assistant coach in the NBA with the San Antonio Spurs.

FARMERS
32
4
DUPREE

Best of the Best

The WNBA has had many top stars. Sue Bird is one of them. Entering the 2019 season, she had played in a record 508 career games. Two other players who put in a lot of time were DeLisha Milton-Jones (499 games) and Tina Thompson (496 games). They each played 17 seasons in the league.

October 5, 2017: Rebekkah Brunson becomes the only player in WNBA history to win five championship titles. She earned one with the Sacramento Monarchs, and four with the Minnesota Lynx.

Tina Thompson was named to the WNBA All-Star Game nine times.

What's Next?

What is the future of the WNBA? We think it will get bigger. In the next few seasons, the league might add one or two more teams. Nashville, Tennessee, could be a WNBA city. We also think Breanna Stewart of the Seattle Storm is going to be the league's biggest star! She was named the league MVP and Finals MVP in 2018. She also helped lead the Storm to the WNBA title. Bad news for opponents: Stewart was only 24 years old in 2019!

In 2019, more WNBA games were on live national TV than ever before. The league hopes to have even more games to watch in the future.

Stewart had to miss the 2019 season with an injury. She planned to be ready to keep scoring in 2020.

SWEDISH
30
verizon

Glossary

center (SEN-ter) the tallest player on a team, she usually plays closest to the basket

decade (DEK-aid) a period of 10 years

dunk (DUNK) a shot in which a player slams or stuffs the ball into the basket

free throw (FREE THROH) a shot from the 15-foot (4.5 m) line awarded to a player after an opponent commits certain types of fouls

guard (GARD) a basketball position that often dribbles and passes as well as shoots

inspired (in-SPY-erd) acted in a way that caused others to try to become better

MVP most valuable player

opponent (uh-POH-nunt) the team that is on the opposite side of your team

pro (PROH) short for "professional," it means playing sports for money

Find Out More

IN THE LIBRARY

Buckley, James Jr. *It's a Numbers Game: Basketball*. Washington, DC: National Geographic Kids, 2020.

Macy, Sue. *Basketball Belles: How Two Teams and One Scrappy Player Put Women's Hoops on the Map*. New York, NY: Holiday House, 2019.

Sports Illustrated Kids. *My First Book of Basketball*. New York, NY: Sports Illustrated Kids, 2018.

ON THE WEB

Visit our Web site for links about WNBA history:

childsworld.com/links

Note to Parents, Teachers, and Librarians: We routinely verify our Web links to make sure they are safe and active sites. So encourage your readers to check them out!

Index

About the Author

Ellen Labrecque has written more than 100 books for children. A former editor at *Sports Illustrated Kids* Magazine, she loves covering and watching the WNBA. She played basketball in college, where she was named to the Academic All-America team. She lives in Bucks County, Pennsylvania, with her husband and two kids.